Horse Gentler
in Training

Winnie
The Early Years

Horse Gentler in Training

Dandi Daley Mackall

illustrated by Phyllis Harris

Tyndale House Publishers, Inc.
Carol Stream, IL

Visit Tyndale's website for kids at www.tyndale.com/kids.

Visit Dandi Daley Mackall online at www.dandibooks.com.

TYNDALE is a registered trademark of Tyndale House Publishers, Inc. The Tyndale Kids logo is a trademark of Tyndale House Publishers, Inc.

Horse Gentler in Training

Designed by Jacqueline L. Nuñez

Edited by Sarah Rubio

Scripture quotations are taken from the *Holy Bible*, New Living Translation, copyright © 1996, 2004, 2015 by Tyndale House Foundation. Used by permission of Tyndale House Publishers, Inc., Carol Stream, Illinois 60188. All rights reserved.

Horse Gentler in Training is a work of fiction. Where real people, events, establishments, organizations, or locales appear, they are used fictitiously. All other elements of the novel are drawn from the author's imagination.

For manufacturing information regarding this product, please call 1-800-323-9400.

For information about special discounts for bulk purchases, please contact Tyndale House Publishers at csresponse@tyndale.com, or call 1-800-323-9400.

Library of Congress Cataloging-in-Publication Data
Names: Mackall, Dandi Daley, author. | Harris, Phyllis, illustrator.
Title: Horse gentler in training / Dandi Daley Mackall ; illustrations by Phyllis Harris.
Description: Carol Stream, Illinois : Tyndale Kids, Tyndale House Publishers, Inc., [2018]
| Summary: Eight-year-old Winnie is determined to become a horse gentler like her mother, both to prove herself to Austin, a big-talking classmate who owns a thoroughbred, and to save the ranch.
Identifiers: LCCN 2018027427 | ISBN 9781496432803 (sc)
Subjects: | CYAC: Christian life—Fiction. | Horses—Training—Fiction. | Ranch life—Wyoming—Fiction. | Wyoming—Fiction.
Classification: LCC PZ7.M1905 Hnq 2018 | DDC [Fic]—dc23 LC record available at https://lccn.loc.gov/2018027427

Printed in the United States of America

24	23	22	21	20	19	18
7	6	5	4	3	2	1

*For Ellie, my granddaughter, who is already on
her way to becoming a horse gentler*

What is impossible for people is possible with God.

LUKE 18:27

Contents

Chapter 1

How Not to Catch a Princess

"Hang on, Winnie!" Mom shouts into the wind as Chief, our sleepy plow horse, plods on.

I wrap my arms around Mom's waist. We're riding double. Bareback. I know what's coming.

Chief trots, making us bounce on his broad back. Then he breaks into a slow canter. He's

1

the oldest horse on the Willis Wyoming Ranch.
I love our ranch, so I can't stop thinking about
the argument I overheard last night:

"Jack, we can't lose the ranch!" Mom said.
"We need to hold on and pray."

"Prayer won't pay the bills, Emily," Dad said.

We board horses, and Mom gentles them.

Other trainers "break" horses, sometimes in cruel ways. Not Mom. She is so good with horses you'd think she was one. It's their owners we have trouble with.

More than anything on earth, I want to be a horse gentler like Mom.

"Uh-oh." Mom eases Chief to a walk.

Mr. Green and his son Austin are in our pasture. Mr. Green is wearing green pants and a green shirt. I've never seen him in any other color. Austin is eight, like his twin, Simon. And me.

Mr. Green runs toward Royal Princess, their new champion Thoroughbred. The mare's deep-brown coat shines in the sunlight. Princess keeps munching grass until Mr. Green is a horse's tail away. Then she trots to the far end of the pasture. "Come back here!" he cries.

"I'll get that horse!" Austin shouts.

Mom slides off Chief and whispers, "Winnie Willis, in the beginning God created heaven and earth and horses. And sometimes I have to wonder if the good Lord shouldn't have quit while he was ahead."

Chapter 2

Teaching Moments

Austin tiptoes behind Princess.

Never a good idea.

Before I can holler, Princess kicks, just missing Austin. He scrambles backward, trips over his own feet, and lands in the dust.

"Austin, what did I tell you about standing behind a horse?" Mom shouts.

Austin jumps up and dusts off his jeans like they're on fire. "Stupid horse!" he mutters.

I feel a teaching moment coming on. That's what Mom calls a talking-to about something that just happened.

Austin won't be easy to "gentle."

"Austin," Mom begins in her gentlest voice. "Horses see all around them, except for blind spots in front and behind. Princess saw you coming at her. Then she lost sight of you. That frightened her, so she kicked."

"You're supposed to tame my horse!" Austin cries. "That's what we pay you for!"

I slide off Chief. He's about 18 hands (or 6 feet) high, a farm horse that came with the farm we turned into our ranch. I'm short. It's a long way down.

Then I get a great idea.

Note to self: Winnie Willis, this is your chance. Call me Winnie the Horse Gentler!

"I got this!" I tell Mom.

"Winnie?"

But she's too late. *I'm* going to catch that horse, or my name isn't Winnie the Horse Gentler!

7

Chapter 3

Catch Me If You Can

"Here, Princess," I whisper.

Princess stops grazing.

"Good girl," I say, loud enough for Austin and his dad to hear. Horses learn by watching horses. Maybe people learn by watching people.

Princess is watching me.

So is Mom.

I whistle, like Mom does. Slowly, I reach for Princess. Thoroughbreds can be nervous and high strung. That quick energy makes them good racehorses. But they can get scared easily. Austin and his dad scared Princess. I know better. Plus, I'm not at all scary.

My hand is almost to her halter.

Princess lets out a whistle of her own, a whinny.

A horse laugh.

She rears, then canters off.

Behind me, I hear human laughter. Austin's.

Mom brushes past me and whistles.

Princess prances up. "Come on, Princess." Mom scratches the horse's neck. Instead of grabbing the halter, she keeps scratching Princess.

Austin and his dad stare as Mom and Princess stroll into the barn.

Note to self: there is only one horse gentler at the Willis Wyoming Ranch. And it's not Winnie.

Chapter 4

Lizzy's Lizard

Austin and his dad storm into the barn after Mom and Princess.

"Can I ride *now*?" Austin shouts, making Princess stir in the cross-ties. We keep leather lead ropes hanging from both sides of the stall way so we can snap the hooks onto the halter from both sides. Horses have nowhere to go when they're in cross-ties.

"Today we'll work on grooming." Mom says grooming a horse is the best way to get to know her.

"What?" Austin sounds like Mom's asking him to eat Princess. "That's *your* job!"

"Next time, please have the horse groomed before our arrival," Mr. Green says.

Mom gives them a big smile. "We'll be using those brushes." She points to the shelf outside the tack room. "And we'll need a hoof pick for cleaning her hooves. It's the small metal thing that looks like a question mark— the red one."

Austin and his dad exchange looks. Then Mr. Green gets the brushes and hoof pick and delivers them to Mom.

Austin crosses his arms in front of him. "I'm

not doing it! We paid for *riding* lessons. Not grooming lessons."

I can't watch. I head for the house.

Lizzy, my little sister, is on her hands and knees, sniffing the ground. She's one day short of a year younger and a whole inch taller than me. We both have Mom's dark hair and green eyes. But Lizzy is scared of horses and loves bugs and lizards almost as much as I

love horses. Our school takes field trips to Lizzy's lizard farm.

Mom says I'm a wild Mustang and Lizzy is a good-natured Trakehner.

"I've lost my only Great Plains Earless," Lizzy explains.

"Need my help?" I ask, hoping she'll say no. The last time I helped her catch a lizard, I freaked out. Plus, I got poison ivy.

Note to self: next time, stay in the stable.

Something swishes behind me. I jump and bump into something. Some*one*. "Sorry, Simon." It's hard to believe Simon and Austin are twins. They both have black hair, but Simon's is really short. He wears glasses and almost always a smile. Austin wears no glasses and no smile.

"That's okay. I'm in the way. Winnie, how are you today?"

There is a reason we call him Rhymin'
Simon.

"Help me find my Earless Lizard?" Lizzy
begs. "Officially, it's called a Great Plains
Earless Lizard. They only showed up in
Wyoming a few years ago. It's not even as
long as my finger. No ear openings, but a big
mouth. The head is kind of funny shaped, like
God forgot to give them chins. White belly.
Stripes on its back. But they're brown and gray,
so that makes them hard to see. I thought I'd
never catch it. Now we have to catch it again!"

Simon drops down next to her. "Can do . . .
for you."

I never feel at ease around Simon. I keep
thinking I should rhyme back. And I'm not a
good rhymer. "See you guys." *Eagle eyes. Just
my size. I'll be wise.*

Note to self: maybe I'm not so bad at rhyming.

As I walk away, I hear Simon: "Lizzy, Lizzy, have no fears. We'll catch this creature with no ears."

I turn back. As Lizzy's big sis, I have a duty to set her straight. "You do know catching the same lizard twice is impossible?"

Lizzy doesn't look up. "Winnie, nothing is impossible with God."

"Even capturing a lizard so odd," Simon adds.

Note to self: I really don't like rhyme.

Chapter 5

Monday, Monday–Not a Fun Day

Monday I catch Dad just as he's leaving for work. He's asking Mom and Lizzy, "How about a remote-controlled shower? You could turn it on from bed, and the water would warm up while you get a few more minutes of sleep." Dad's always thinking up crazy inventions.

Mom kisses Dad's cheek. "Someday you'll have to quit selling insurance and make these inventions yourself."

"What would they do with Dad's billboards if he quit?" I ask. Dad's the boss of Best Bet Insurance. They put his face on two billboards, so he's kind of famous.

"I'm sure they'd think of something," Mom says.

"Dad? Can you please get home before bedtime tonight?" Even I can hear the whine in my voice.

Dad kisses the top of my head. "I promise to be home before bedtime, Winnie," he says. "*My* bedtime."

"Not funny, Dad," Lizzy says.

Dad kisses Lizzy's head too. "Don't miss the bus, girls."

I like my teacher. If Miss Pento were a horse, she'd be a frisky Welsh Pony. They're small, but they can do anything—jump, dressage, pull a cart, or trail ride.

Miss Pento pulls her blonde hair into a ponytail. "Class, let's share your answers to the journal question: 'What did you do this weekend?'"

I forgot all about this. And I'm supposed to have such a great memory. Dad says I have a photographic memory, so I should have a better report card. I tried to explain that my brain takes pictures without me, and I can't help if it doesn't like math pictures.

Landri goes first. She looks enough like our teacher to be her kid. She'd be a Palomino yearling if she were a horse. Her creamy blonde hair is exactly the right color for a Palomino. "I had ballet with Ellie and Maddie and Cassie," she begins. "I went to church. Then we watched boring sports on TV."

We all clap for Landri, partly because she did such a good job but mostly because we like her.

Simon's presentations are usually unusual. "You'd hardly believe what a weekend I had. It started out fine. Then the day became sad. A lizard was lost. My brother got mad. And now I am done—too bad."

Even Miss Pento looks confused. "Well, Simon, that was very . . . rhyming."

Ellie tells what she read and what she drew and which crafts she worked on. Brooks tells what he ate. Seth played sports. Tamson claims she won everything, from board games to races.

When it's Austin's turn, he struts up front. "We saved the best for last!"

So Austin hasn't noticed *I'm* last. Maybe Miss Pento won't notice either.

"You guys told us what you did this week-end," Austin begins. "Boring! *I'm* going to tell you what I *didn't* do!" He gives me a look that makes me feel like losing my breakfast.

Note to self: this won't be good.

Chapter 6

Big Talker

"I got a really expensive horse," Austin begins.

Landri asks, "Was it your birthday?"

Austin's face wrinkles like he doesn't get the question. "No. Why?"

Landri's face turns pink. "Well, I just thought a horse would make a really good birthday gift, and maybe—"

"I got the horse because I wanted a champion," Austin interrupts. "My horse's father was a champion racehorse and ran in the Kentucky Derby. He only won third place. But that was the jockey's fault. *My* horse will win first place. Dad says Royal Princess cost more than the car he bought Mom for Christmas."

Note to self: Austin Green is a big talker.

Austin keeps bragging until Miss Pento interrupts. "Thank you, Austin."

He frowns at her. "I'm not done! Remember? I said I was going to talk about what I *didn't* do last weekend. So we take Royal Princess to the Willis ranch. They do the dirty work, like cleaning the stall. I got the horse so I could ride in shows and win trophies. But did I get to ride? NO! Why not?"

I feel boiling lava start in my toes and move to my face.

Austin glares at me. "Because certain people didn't do their jobs! They took the money to break my horse, and they expect me to—"

The lava explodes inside me. "*Break* your horse? You don't know anything about horses!"

"Like you do?" Austin says.

Usually, I know exactly what kind of horse a person would be. Austin could never be a horse. Not in a million years.

"We don't break horses!" I explain.

Austin smirks. "No kidding."

His buddies laugh.

"We don't break a horse's spirit. Mom and I gentle horses."

Miss Pento swishes her ponytail. "Gentle them? How does that work?"

"It doesn't!" Austin snaps. "She can't even catch my horse."

I storm up the aisle before Miss Pento can stop me. "I can too catch your horse!"

"Winnie?" Miss Pento steps from behind her desk. "It's still Austin's turn."

"I told Dad he should fire your mom," Austin snaps.

TEST TOMORROW

"Oh yeah?" All I know is that Mom can't get fired and that I'm so mad at Austin that if I were a horse, I'd bite him.

Austin fake laughs. "I'm done, Miss Pento," he says. "It's Winnie's turn to tell us what she did over the weekend. More like what she *didn't* do."

"All right, Winnie. What did you do this weekend?" Miss Pento asks.

I'm in front of the class, alone. "I worked on catching Princess."

Brooks, who is nice for a boy, asks, "What else do you do with Austin's horse?"

I could say I brush Princess, feed her, clean out her hooves, and muck her stall. But that doesn't sound like much. "Ride her." That's what I *would* do if I could catch her, if Mom says it's okay, if—

"Cool!" Brooks turns to Austin. "So Winnie can ride your horse, but you can't?"

As I walk to the back row, I hear Ellie whisper, "That's so cool!"

Landri says, "I didn't know you were so good with horses, Winnie."

Austin glances at me, then says something to his buddies.

"How exciting!" Miss Pento exclaims. "You'll have to keep us updated, Winnie. You, too, Austin."

Austin sneers at me. "Count on it."

I slide into my seat.

Note to self: Austin Green is not the only big talker.

Chapter 7

Ride 'Em, Cowgirl?

After school, I run to the bus and sit behind Lizzy and Simon. Simon keeps reading, but Lizzy takes one look at me and asks, "Rough day, Winnie?"

"You could say that again."

"Please help Winnie feel better." Lizzy says this to God with her eyes open. She's always praying before we realize who she's talking to. Mom does the same thing.

I'm really sorry about bragging with a lie mixed in. I say this to God, too. Only the prayer stays inside my head. God still hears it in there.

Our bus jerks forward, then stops. There's a rumble and a squeak, and the old bus shakes to life. Our driver, Mr. Ted, only started driving buses this year. If he were a horse, he'd be a Shetland Pony. He has to sit on a pillow to see the road. Plus, he's as moody as a Shetland. Those ponies can be sweet friends. They can also buck and bite without warning.

"Guess what Simon's reading," Lizzy says.

"A book," I guess.

"A magic book!" Lizzy says. "Magic tricks with coins, boxes, scarves . . . Not real magic."

Simon stops reading. "How's Princess? How's that ride?" He whispers the last line of his rhyme so only I can hear: "Austin thinks that Winnie lied."

I hardly notice when the bus pulls up at our stop. When I step down, I see that Mr. Ted knocked over the school bus stop sign. Again.

Austin is the first kid off. "Bumpy ride, Bus-Ted!" Austin laughs at his own joke. "Get it? Bus-Ted? Busted!" He's still chuckling as he heads for home, not waiting for his brother.

Lizzy gets off behind me. "Thanks for the ride, Mr. Ted," she says.

Simon hops off after Lizzy. He goes left, and we go right.

"Lizzy!" he calls back. "I'll come by in a while. What I bring will make you smile."

"Yay!" Lizzy shouts back. "See you, Simon."

Lizzy and I walk home together. "You sure you're okay?" she asks.

"Austin says they might take Princess to another stable, Lizzy."

"Maybe that wouldn't be so bad," she says.

I turn and look at her. "Are you kidding? It would be awful!"

"Don't worry, Winnie. God's got this. He knows everything."

Not a comforting thought right now. I picture Jesus shaking his head as I brag about riding Princess.

But what if I really do ride Princess? I was riding horses before I could walk. And if I really ride Princess, then my lie wasn't totally a lie. I *can* ride Royal Princess.

Note to self: do it!

As soon as Lizzy and I get home, Mom makes us do homework, then heads for the garden.

"Simon might come over later," Lizzy says.

"Good. I like that boy." Mom grins. "He's filled with joy."

I groan.

Simon is waiting for us outside. He hands Lizzy something squirmy. It's round with short legs.

"Oh, Winnie, look!" Lizzy takes the ugly, squirmy thing from Simon.

"Don't tell me you're starting a toad farm," I plead.

"It's not a toad, silly," Lizzy says. "You're looking at Wyoming's state reptile, the Horned Lizard!"

Simon's grin takes up his whole face. "Some folks call him a Horned Toad. I found him on a country road."

"But they'd be wrong," Lizzy explains, petting the creature. "He's part of the iguana family. Simon, he's wonderful! Thank you! I think I'll call him Bug."

Leaving Lizzy with Bug, and Mom with weeds, I trot to the pasture. When I whistle, Chief comes lumbering over. I scratch his cheek. Every horse has a favorite scratching spot, and Chief's is definitely his cheek. Chief was probably browner when he was young, though never as shiny brown as Princess. The old plow horse's coat must have faded with age. Horses can get sunburned, and too much sunshine has speckled the brown hairs over Chief's back. His mane and tail are thin compared to Princess's. But I like his giant hooves, except when he accidentally steps on me.

Princess is waiting for me in her stall. I don't even have to catch her.

I give her a quick brushing and bridle her. "I've never ridden a champion," I tell her. "No time for a saddle. Besides, Austin's saddle is too fancy. And I love riding bareback." When I ride bareback, I can feel what a horse is going to do before she does it. I love being as close as I can to a horse.

I can't wait to tell Austin that I've ridden Princess—for real.

Plus, Mom will have to admit I'm an honest-to-goodness horse gentler.

The only hard part about riding without a

saddle is getting up on a horse's back. I lead Princess to the step stool in the pasture. Some of our riders use it to reach the stirrup when they mount. Mom makes kids ride with saddles for lessons, and that's the way they like it anyway.

Princess plants her hooves and refuses to go closer.

"Come on, Princess." My voice is gentle, like Mom's.

Princess shies away from the stool a couple of times before finally standing still.

It takes three tries, but with a little jump, I make it onto her back.

I am on Austin Green's horse! I did it! Now all I have to do is—

Princess starts dancing in place.

I grab a handful of mane. "Easy, Princess." I squeeze with my legs—gently—to urge her into a walk.

Princess bolts.

"Whoa!" I cry as her mane slips through my fingers.

She rears. I slip back. She bucks.

The last thing I see is Princess's tail as she runs off and I'm catapulted up, up, up into the sky.

Chapter 8

Ouch!

There is a point in my flight where I stop going up.

Then down,
      down,
            down. *Thunk!*

Princess gallops away. Without me.

I hear footsteps. Voices.

"Winnie!" Lizzy shrieks. "Please, Lord, let
my sister be okay!"

Lizzy and Simon squat beside me. They look so scared that now *I'm* super scared.

"What happened?" Lizzy demands.

"A-OK?" Simon says. "Please say."

I sit up. "I guess."

"Thank you!" Lizzy says, probably to God.

I agree.

Simon stretches out a hand to help me up. I take his hand. He pulls.

"OUCH!" I sit back down. Simon backs off.

"What?" Lizzy cries.

"My wrist." I'm trying to hold back tears.

"I'll get Mom!" Lizzy races off.

Simon is staring at me like I'm a horror movie. "Sorry."

I wait for the rest, wondering what rhymes with *sorry*.

The rhyme doesn't come.

Note to self: I must be worse off than I thought.

Dinner at the Willises' kitchen table is silent. Mom called Dad, and he had to leave work early to meet us at the emergency room.

When Mom came to my rescue, I thought about telling her I slipped and fell. I did slip—off of Princess. And I fell.

But that would have been just a fancy lie. And lying got me into this mess.

The emergency room doctor said my wrist is *just* sprained. But he put my arm in a sling so I wouldn't use it.

I have been trying—and failing—to eat corn left-handed since we sat down to supper. I drop my fork. "This is impossible."

Dad harrumphs. "I'll tell you what's impossible. Keeping this ranch going."

Mom sets down her fork. "That's not true, Jack. We should be able to pay that feed bill by the end of the month, thanks to the

Greens. Father, thanks for sending the Greens to us."

Mom doesn't call Dad "Father," so I know she's slipped into a prayer.

"The Greens?" Dad says. "Mr. Green phoned me at the office. He's taking his horse somewhere else unless there's more progress."

If Mom were a horse, her ears would be flat back in anger, and her nostrils would flare. "Can't he talk to *me*? I have half a mind to kick him and his horse off the ranch!"

"Great," Dad says. "Then it really will be impossible to save the ranch."

I wait for Lizzy to remind us about nothing being impossible with God.

Dad isn't finished. "And now, thanks to Winnie, you'll have to do everything your-self—your chores *and* her chores."

I wince like I've been hit. I hadn't thought about how having my arm in a sling would make life harder for Mom. Suddenly, I don't feel like eating.

Dad takes his last bite of meat loaf and mutters, "Impossible."

When Lizzy still doesn't chime in, I elbow her.

Lizzy is staring at her plate. I know my sister well enough to know she's praying.

Even Lizzy realizes we're in trouble.

Note to self: this is all my fault.

Chapter 9

Very Tricky

School is harder left-handed. My journal looks like a chicken danced in it. I have to sit out in gym because we play gaga ball. And you need a good wrist for that one. I don't go out at recess because Miss Pento is afraid I'll fall and hurt my wrist.

Plus, everybody knows I fell off Austin's

horse. Austin claims if they don't see progress by the weekend, they're moving Princess to the Triple Bar Ranch in Laramie, where they punish horses to break their spirits.

Wednesday, Simon walks home with Lizzy and me. I can't stop complaining about Simon's brother. "Sorry, Simon. I just don't want Austin to move Princess from our ranch. And I can't do anything about it."

Simon sticks his book, *Millions of Marvelous Magic Tricks*, in my face. He wiggles his eyebrows. "If you need an answer quick, you could always try a trick."

Note to self: well, I'll be a Horned Toad! That's it!

At home, I beg Mom to let me go to the barn.

"Yes," she says, making it sound like no. "But no riding, no leading, no sitting on any horse."

"Got it." I take off for the barn. If I had more time, I could go to the library. Maybe they'd have books on teaching horses tricks. But I don't have time. I need to teach Princess a trick by Friday.

I brush Princess one-handed. I stroke her all over and find her sweet spots. She loves being scratched where Mom scratched her, under the mane. But I find another favorite spot. When I rub behind her ear, her eyes close and she tilts her head closer to me.

"Let's shake hands, Princess." I remember seeing a TV show where the horse could shake hands. I reach for her foreleg with my good hand.

Princess eyes me and takes a couple of steps back.

I run my hand down her leg. "Shake?"

Her hoof stays planted.

I stroke her foreleg again and press my fingers to her pastern, the part of the lower leg between the fetlock and hoof, kind of where an ankle would be.

No go. I try the other foreleg. No luck there, either.

For over an hour, I try and try. Twice, Princess lifts her leg. But she thinks I want to clean out her hoof.

This is not working.

Thursday after school, I race home and try the handshake trick again.

Once again, I fail.

I rub behind her ear. "Princess, they're coming *tomorrow*."

Without warning, Princess bobs her head, nose to chest. I shoo the pesky fly that was bothering her.

The fly returns. Princess bobs her head again.

I flick the fly away. Then I get an idea. I barely touch Princess's chest, just like that fly.

Yes! Princess nods.

"That's it! Princess, do you like me?"

I touch her chest. She bobs her nose to her chest and answers *yes*.

"Do you want to stay with us at the Willis Wyoming Ranch?"

She answers *yes*.

I laugh. It feels like Princess is laughing too. But this time, it's a good laugh.

We practice until all I have to do is point to her chest to get a *yes*.

It's getting dark, but I can't quit. Every *yes* needs a *no*. I've seen horses shake their heads to get rid of flies.

It takes a lot of touching and talking, but I find a sensitive spot under the mane. After more practice, Princess shakes her head *no* when I lightly touch the spot.

I run through a bunch of *no* questions and answers. Princess is perfect. I can't wait to show Austin and his dad.

Note to self: and Mom.

Chapter 10

Trick or Treat

On Friday the doctor gives me one more day
with the sling if I keep my wrist bandaged. It's
all I can do not to tell Landri and Ellie about
Princess's tricks. It's a long day, and I'm glad
when school ends.

On the bus ride home, Simon is still reading his magic tricks book. He's on the last

chapter: "Locks." When we're almost to our stop, I ask, "Simon, are you coming over later, with Austin?"

"Wouldn't miss it. I'll be there. So will Dad, so best beware."

Princess nickers when I walk into the barn for some last-minute practice. A soft, sweet nicker.

"I'm glad to see you, too, girl," I say. So far, I haven't blown into Princess's nostrils, the way horses greet each other. But since she's given me her first nicker, I try it. She doesn't blow back, but her ears flick up, and she lowers her head. We're getting to be friends.

I climb into the stall with her. She gets my best one-handed brushing. Then I scratch her in her favorite spots. "Time for business now, Princess. Austin and his dad will be here before long."

I hear a truck outside. "Can't be the Greens this early," I tell Princess.

I take a peek just in time to see a green car, pulling a green horse trailer. It *is* the Greens!

Our screen door slaps. Mom comes out, hands on hips. "Evening, Mr. Green." She strolls to the trailer. "Interesting choice of vehicles."

"Be prepared, I always say," says Mr. Green. "We've come to talk over our options concerning Austin's horse."

"Yeah." Austin steps out of the car. He's wearing fancy boots with the worst kind of silver spurs—wheels of sharp little daggers.

I want to tell Austin that I won't let him near Princess with those spurs. But I'm waiting for Mom to say something.

Simon climbs out, and Lizzy appears from

the backyard. She runs up to Simon and whispers something. They both look worried.

"You won't be needing that trailer, Mr. Green," I announce.

Mr. Green perks up and looks to Mom. "You've made progress?"

Mom explains, "Princess is still getting used to us. I haven't ridden her yet because I felt she wasn't ready. I'll ride her tomorrow before you come. Then I'll know when to let Austin ride."

"See, Dad? They haven't done anything! Let's take Princess to Laramie." Austin points to my sling. "She's no help."

"Oh yeah?" I take a deep breath. "Princess and I have something to show you."

Mom frowns. "Winnie?"

Mr. Green looks at me like he feels sorry for me. "Really, dear?"

"Really." I lead them to Princess's stall, and I go in. Simon and Lizzy crowd closer, and I'm glad they're here. I should have told Simon thanks for the hint about tricks. But I couldn't think of anything good that rhymes with *thanks.*

"Waste of time," Austin grumbles.

I send up a quick prayer for Princess. For our ranch. And for me. "Princess, are you making progress?"

Blocking Austin and his dad's view with my sling, I touch Princess's chest.

She nods *yes*.

Mr. Green's eyebrows shoot up.

I keep going, like I'm not at all surprised. But inside, I'm thanking God and asking him to keep it up. "Princess, are you having a good time at the Willis Wyoming Ranch?"

Again, she nods *yes*.

"Well, that *is* something," Mr. Green admits.

"No, it isn't!" Austin steps closer. "Let *me* ask the questions."

"Go right ahead, Austin." My heart is pounding, but I manage a smile.

Austin steps a little closer but stays out of the stall. "Princess, do you want to leave this dump?" He sneers like he's got me now.

Keeping my gaze on Austin, I touch Princess's neck. She shakes her head *no*.

"Wait," Austin says. "Okay, horse. Do you like me better than Winnie?"

Princess shakes her head *no*.

Austin frowns. "Do you like Winnie better than me?"

Yes, Princess answers.

Mr. Green bursts out laughing. "Well, I've seen enough for now. That's quite a show, young lady."

"Dad!" Austin shouts, running after Mr. Green, who's returning to the trailer. "I still can't ride my own horse! That Laramie guy said he'd have me riding in 24 hours."

"I know, son." He opens the driver's door, then looks to Mom. "We're leaving without the horse. For tonight. Tomorrow is another story. I'm going to need to see more."

We watch them drive away. I'm thankful they're gone. But I'm scared about tomorrow.

Mom puts her arm around my shoulder. "Nice job, Winnie."

Any other time, it would feel like heaven to hear Mom say I'd done a nice job with a horse. But she sounds as worried about tomorrow as I am.

Chapter 11

Try, Try Again

Saturday, before dawn, I ditch my sling and run to the barn. My wrist still hurts, but I have more important things on my mind. Overnight, I got another idea, thanks to Simon's trick book.

Princess is restless while I groom her. I keep talking to her. "So, Simon was reading about locks. That gave me our new trick. You're going to learn to unlock locks! All locks on the ranch are the same. You just lift the bar. Simple!"

It doesn't take long to discover locks are *not* simple. Not when you have to use hooves or a big horse nose.

I try everything. I hold a handful of oats under the lock. I sprinkle oats on the lock bar. I unlock it with *my* nose.

Nothing works.

I trudge back to the house.

Mom points to my sling-less arm. "How's the wrist?"

"Okay. The rest of me, not so much. I tried to teach Princess a new trick so they'd give us more time. But it didn't work."

Mom puts her hands on my shoulders. "Sweetheart, it's okay."

I fight back tears, remembering how Mom told me I'd done a good job.

"Winnie, Princess's progress didn't come from tricks. She's better because you're spending time with her. She trusts you. That's a wonderful first step. I'll ride her after breakfast, and we'll see where we are."

A scream from the backyard sends us running to the rescue.

Lizzy is staring at her lizard farm. "Bug is gone!"

I want to go back to Princess. But Lizzy needs me. "I'll help. We'll find Bug."

The three of us are still searching for Bug when I hear the Green's truck and trailer.

"They're early, Mom!" I cry. "You haven't ridden Princess yet!"

Simon is first out of the truck. I send him to help Lizzy.

Mom joins Mr. Green. "I wasn't expecting you this early."

I race to the barn, down the stall way,
straight to Princess's stall.

I stop running.

Then I stop breathing.

I am staring at an empty stall.

Royal Princess is gone.

Chapter 12

Disappearing Act

Maybe someone let Princess out. I dash to the pasture. The only horse there is Chief.

"Winnie?" Mom's voice makes me spin around. "Why is the gate open?"

I see that the pasture gate is wide open too.

"Where's my horse?" Austin demands.

Mr. Green scowls. "Is Princess in the barn?"

Austin heads for the barn. "That horse better be ready to ride!"

Mom is frowning at me. "Winnie?"

Austin stomps back from the barn. "What did you do with my horse?"

Mom runs and looks for herself. "Winnie, what's going on?"

"I don't know, Mom! Princess was gone when I came out!"

"That horse is worth a fortune!" Mr. Green shouts. "I'm holding you responsible!"

Mom manages to keep her voice gentle. "Who else knows that your horse is worth a fortune?"

"Everybody," I answer. "Austin brags about it all the time."

"I'm calling the sheriff," Mr. Green says.

Something hits me with the force of a horseshoe to my head. *Princess unlocked the gates!*

And I'm the one who taught her. For a second, I think about keeping quiet. It wouldn't be lying. *I* didn't say someone stole her.

But . . . I'm tired of my not-quite-lies. They are still lies.

"It's my fault," I say. "And I'm going to find Princess and bring her back."

I leave them standing there as I race from the pasture.

Simon and Lizzy are at the gate. "We'll look this way!" Lizzy points right.

I nod and go left.

When I reach the dense woods, I'm out of breath. "Please help me find Princess!" I surprise myself by praying out loud.

I half expect to see Princess when I open my eyes. She isn't there. But my heart isn't pounding anymore. I feel calm.

Gentle.

A few minutes later, I stop. I sniff. I smell *horse*! Horse is the best smell on earth.

I follow my nose. Between two pines, I see Princess, standing stiff and scared.

"Hey, Princess." I use my gentle voice. "You need to come home." I stay where I am and prepare to whistle.

Princess nods, then takes a few steps toward me.

We meet in the middle. "Good girl, Princess. You're so smart. I guess that last trick was on me."

I lead her back through the woods.

We're almost out when I see something wiggling through the pine needles ahead. I stop so fast that Princess bumps into me. *Snake?*

Then I see it. A lizard. I'm pretty sure it's Bug. I'd almost rather see a snake. The last thing I want to do is touch that yucky creature.

But Lizzy's out looking for a horse, and she's scared of horses.

I reach down and sweep Bug up in my good hand. That leaves my bad wrist for Princess. And my wrist hurts.

Princess nudges me with her soft nose. When I walk on, so does she. She trails behind me all the way home.

Lizzy comes running. "You found Bug!"

I gladly hand over the lizard. Then I walk Princess into the pasture.

Mom, Austin, and Mr. Green join us at the gate.

"Good job, Winnie!" Mom pushes the gate shut and locks it.

"We still don't know how the horse got out," Mr. Green complains.

"*I* know!" Austin says. "Winnie left the gates open. She just doesn't want to admit it."

Mom looks at me, and the question is on her face.

I shake my head. "I didn't leave it unlocked. Princess did."

"Sure," Austin says. "Blame my horse."

"I blame myself." I'm still calm and gentle. "*I* taught her to unlock locks."

"No way!" Austin shouts, making Princess back off. "Just because you got her to say yes and no? You think we're going to believe that my horse unlocked those gates?"

Mom bursts out laughing. She points to Princess, who is at the gate, pressing her nose against the lock.

We watch as Princess unlocks the gate.

I jog over to her.

Austin is right behind me. "How is that even possible?" he mutters.

I rub Princess's ear. "Nothing is impossible with God. Right, Princess?"

Princess bobs her head up and down. *Yes!*

Chapter 13

All's Well That Ends Well

Lizzy and I follow Dad to the mailbox. It feels like a parade, a celebration.

"I'm still not sure how your mother pulled this off," Dad says. "But Mr. Green paid three months of boarding fees in advance." He waves a fistful of envelopes in the air, then drops them into the box. "As of now, all bills for the Willis Wyoming Ranch are paid in full!"

Lizzy raises the tiny red flag on our mailbox

so the mail lady will pick up our bills. "I knew you'd come through, God. No worries." She brushes a fly from her arm.

Dad shoos another fly about to land. "I guess I'm going to have to start worrying less and praying more. Wouldn't you say so, Winnie?" When I don't answer right away, he says, "What are you looking at?"

I point to the pasture. Mom is riding Princess while Chief looks on, swishing his tail to fight the flies. Dad and Lizzy follow me to the fence for a better view.

"Princess is loving it as much as Mom," I say.

"How can you tell?" Lizzy asks.

It's hard to explain, but I try. "She's got joy in her ears." Princess's ears are straight forward, with an occasional flick back to listen to Mom.

"Winnie," Dad says, "you and your mom love to ride. I'll give you that. But you can't tell me horses love to have humans on their backs. That's impossible."

Lizzy sighs. "Nothing's impossible—"

"—with God," I finish. "Hey, Princess!"

I shout. Mom and Princess stop and turn to us. "Do you love to ride?"

We wait. I'm hoping a fly will land on Princess the way flies have been landing on us.

"Doesn't look like she's going to give you an answer," Dad says.

I ask again. "Princess, do you love being ridden?"

Chief nickers. And when we all turn to him, he dips his head to his chest: *Yes!*

~~Note to self:~~ *Note to God: thanks for making all things possible.*

My Misty was the sweetest, most wonderful horse a kid could have. We were never sure of his breed, but I always considered him a pure black Morgan. Misty had a Morgan's

calm, trustworthy nature and good sense.
Our house formed one side of the fenced area
where Misty stayed when he wasn't out in the
pasture. So in the morning I could open my
window, and Misty would stick in his beautiful
head to say hello. After school, I'd race home
and climb the top rung of the fence so Misty
could meet me and lay his head in my lap
for a good scratching and the apple I'd saved
from lunch. I really did teach my horse to say
yes and no, much as Winnie teaches Princess
in this book. Misty proved that a horse can
definitely be a kid's best friend.

Fun Horse Facts

- Horses have the largest eyes of any land mammal. They can see almost all the way around themselves. But horses do have blind spots directly in front and behind. That's why if you come up behind a horse, you might startle it, and you might get kicked.

- People used to think that horses were color blind. They aren't—but they do see yellow and green better than purple.

- A horse can see better at night than a human can.

- Adult female horses (mares) usually have 36 to 40 teeth, and adult males have 40 to 44. You can guess a horse's age by looking at its teeth.

- Some horses have extra teeth called wolf teeth, usually on the upper jaw. Most vets will pull them out to prevent problems and discomfort.

- Floating a horse's teeth means to file them flat and smooth so chewing is easier. Sharp teeth can cut the inside of a horse's mouth. A float is the type of file used.

- Horses with pink skin can get a sunburn. Black horses can turn brownish red if they get too much sun.

- Horses have around 205 bones.

- An unborn foal usually grows inside its mother for about 340 days, but it can take just over a year. A very short while after birth, the foal can stand and run on its long, wobbly legs.

Horse Terms

Foal—A newborn or very young horse, male or female.

Filly—A young female horse up to four years old.

Horse Colt (or colt)—A young male horse up to four years old. The word *colt* is sometimes used casually to refer to any young horse, male or female.

Yearling—A year-old filly or colt.

Mare—A mature female horse, usually age five or older.

Broodmare—A mare used only for breeding (having foals).

Stallion—A male horse that hasn't had the gelding's surgery. Can be a foal's dad.

Gelding—A male horse that has been gelded (fixed) so he can't mate or be a dad.

Dam—The female parent of a foal (the mom).

Sire—The male parent of a foal (the dad).

Common Horse Breeds

American Saddlebred—These fancy, showy horses are beautiful to watch and are considered gaited horses—three-gaited and five-gaited. The three-gaited horse high steps in a walk, a trot, and a canter. A five-gaited horse adds two other movements: a slow gait, which is a four-beat slow prancing, and a rack, a full-speed, all-out, four-beat gait.

Appaloosa—Appys are easily identified by their spots, and no two horses' spots are exactly the same. Leopard Appaloosas are white all over with dark spots.

Snowflake Appaloosas are dark all over with white spots. Blanket Appaloosas usually have a dark body with dark spots on a white back and hindquarters. Marble Appys have dark, spotted coats that fade as they grow older. This American breed came to us through the Nez Perce Indians. Today, Appaloosas are popular for riding and ranch work. They're known for their sweet nature and a smooth ride.

Arabian—Arabians are thought to be the oldest purebred horse breed in the world. They are elegant and spirited but eager to learn. Winnie dreams of one day owning a beautiful Arabian.

Morgan—When the US Army chose a breed of mounts, they selected Morgan horses for their good natures and hardworking athleticism. Today's Morgan is spirited, intelligent, hardy, strong, and the ideal family horse. All Morgan horses can be traced back to a single horse owned by a man named Justin Morgan. Morgans are usually a solid color—black, brown, bay, or chestnut.

Mustang—Mustang herds came to the United States with Spanish settlers in the 16th century. Some of the horses escaped from ranches and formed herds in the wild. Today's Mustangs are considered feral, or partially wild. There aren't many Mustangs left, so the government tries to protect them. Mustangs are tough and hardy, with solid legs and strong hooves. They can be fast, and they can be stubborn, but they're agile and have great horse sense.

Winnie's mom calls Winnie a Mustang because she's agile, has good sense (most of the time), and can be a bit stubborn.

Quarter Horse—The Quarter Horse is an American breed, loved by cowboys and nearly all riders. Their strong hindquarters help make them the fastest horse in the world for a quarter-mile race. They can herd cattle, turn on a dime, compete in barrel racing, or take you on a safe ride. Quarter Horses are intelligent and easy to gentle.

Thoroughbred—Thoroughbred horses may be the most famous in the world. People everywhere watch races like the Kentucky Derby and cheer for their favorite racehorse. Thoroughbreds are often racehorses because they are the fastest and most expensive breed. Usually a solid color, they are tall and muscular, with gorgeous, refined heads. They tend to be high spirited and aggressive. In this book, Austin Green's horse is a champion Thoroughbred.

Trakehner—These middleweight hunters have terrific confirmation (build)—perfect for dressage and show jumping. Breeders combined the good temperament of the Arabian, the speed and agility of the Thoroughbred, and the strength of the 13th century Prussian Schweiken (ridden by Teutonic knights) to come up with the ideal riding horse, the Trakehner. Winnie's mother says Winnie's sister, Lizzy, is like a Trakehner because she's easygoing, agile, and strong.

Parts of the Horse

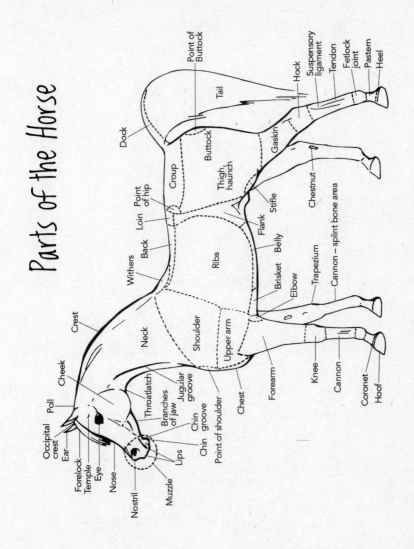

About the Author

Dandi Daley Mackall is the award-winning author of about 500 books for children and adults. She visits countless schools, conducts writing assemblies and workshops across the United States, and presents keynote addresses at conferences and events for young authors. She is also a frequent guest on radio talk shows and has made dozens of appearances on TV. She has won several awards for her writing, including the Helen Keating Ott Award for Outstanding Contribution to Children's Literature and the Edgar Award, and is a two-time winner of the Christian Book Award and the Mom's Choice Award.

Dandi writes from rural Ohio, where she lives with her husband, surrounded by their three children, four granddaughters, and a host of animals. Visit her at www.DandiBooks.com and www.facebook.com/dandi.mackall.

Join twelve-year-old Winnie Willis and her friends—
both human and animal—on their adventures through
paddock and pasture as they learn about caring for
others, trusting God, and growing up.

S·T·A·R·L·I·G·H·T

Animal Rescue

More than just animals need rescuing in this series. Starlight Animal Rescue is where problem horses are trained and loved, where abandoned dogs become heroes, where stray cats become loyal companions—and where people with nowhere to fit in find a place to belong.

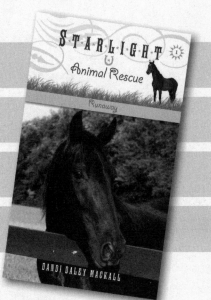

#1 *Runaway*

#2 *Mad Dog*

#3 *Wild Cat*

#4 *Dark Horse*

Read all four to discover how a group of teens cope with life and disappointment.

WWW.TYNDALEKIDS.COM

CP0264

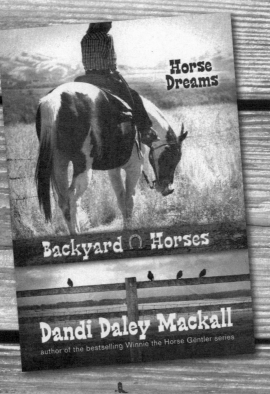